STAND TALL, MOLLY LOU MELON

To my brother J. Christopher Lovell—Merry Christmas 1976;
and, always, to my mother, Sandra
—P. L.

For Emily Anne, the biggest little girl in the neighborhood
—D. C.

WRITTEN BY **PATTY LOVELL** ILLUSTRATED BY **DAVID CATROW**

SCHOLASTIC INC.

New York Toronto London Auckland Sydney
Mexico City New Delhi Hong Kong Buenos Aires

ISBN 0-439-43452-1

Text copyright © 2001 by Patty Lovell.
Illustrations copyright © 2001 by David
Catrow. All rights reserved. Published by
Scholastic Inc., 557 Broadway, New York,
NY 10012, by arrangement with G. P.
Putnam's Sons, a member of Penguin Putnam
Books for Young Readers. SCHOLASTIC and
associated logos are trademarks and/or registered
trademarks of Scholastic Inc.

12 11 10 9 8 7 6 5   2 3 4 5 6 7/0

Printed in the U.S.A.   24

First Scholastic printing, September 2002

Designed by Gina DiMassi.
Text set in Stempel Schneidler medium.

The art was done in pencil and watercolor.

Molly Lou Melon stood just taller than her dog and was the shortest girl in the first grade. She didn't mind. Her grandma had told her, "Walk as proudly as you can and the world will look up to you."

So she did.

Molly Lou Melon had buck teeth that stuck out so far, she could stack pennies on them. She didn't mind. Her grandma had told her, "Smile big and the world will smile right alongside you."

So she did.

Molly Lou Melon had a voice
that sounded like a bullfrog being
squeezed by a boa constrictor.
She didn't mind. Her grandma
had told her, "Sing out clear
and strong and the world will
cry tears of joy."

So she did.

Molly Lou Melon was often fumble fingered.
She didn't mind. Her grandma had told her,
"Believe in yourself and the world will believe
in you too."

So she did.

Then Molly Lou Melon moved to a new town. She had to say good-bye to her grandma and all of her friends . . .

and start in a new school.

On the first day of school, Ronald Durkin
called her "**SHRIMPO!**" in gym class.

When the game started, Molly Lou Melon
caught the football, ran under the legs of
Ronald Durkin, and scored a touchdown.
All the children thought, "Wow, she's good!"
and Ronald Durkin felt very foolish.

On the second day of school, Ronald Durkin called her "**BUCKY-TOOTH BEAVER!**"

Molly Lou Melon took out her pennies, stacked ten high on her teeth, and smiled as big as day. All the children smiled with glee and Ronald Durkin felt very foolish.

On the third day of school, Ronald Durkin said, "You sound like a sick duck—**HONK HONK!**"

Molly Lou Melon sang out a "**QUACK!**" so clear and strong that it made Ronald Durkin somersault backwards, hit his head, and have to go to the nurse. All the children cried with joy to be free of Ronald Durkin for the rest of the afternoon and Ronald Durkin felt very foolish.

On the fourth day of school, Ronald Durkin said that she'd made the snowflake all wrong. But Molly Lou Melon opened up her paper and revealed the most beautiful snowflake of all.

All the children oohed and aahed, even Ronald.

On the fifth day of school, Ronald Durkin
brought Molly Lou Melon a stacking penny
for her tooth and smiled at her.